Enchanted
TALES

PETER HADDOCK PUBLISHING

Contents

The Three Brave Princesses

here was once a king who lived in a castle by the sea with his three lovely daughters. Each of the princesses had a special gift. The eldest daughter could play the fiddle and sing enchanting songs: she could charm the birds from the trees and the beasts from their lairs.

The middle princess had needle-sharp senses: no flower bloomed, no pin dropped and no mouse ran in the grass but this princess could smell, hear and see them from many miles away.

The youngest princess had great skill with a bow: her aim was deadly and no enemy would dare to attack the castle for fear of her arrows.

Besides all these gifts the princesses had one thing in common; they all loved the sea. They were skilled sailors and could navigate by the stars.

You might think that the King was proud of his three gifted daughters, but this was not the case. His love and attention were devoted to a magic apple tree. Every night the tree produced a crop of glittering golden apples, its branches hanging low with the weight of them. In the morning it was the task of the King's daughters to gather the precious fruit in baskets and carry it to their father. He would rub his hands in glee and dismiss the princesses without so much as a "thank you". Though he was a king, he was the servant of the magic tree and thought of nothing else. He spent every day polishing its green leaves and suffered torment if one of them fell.

One morning when the three princesses went to gather the golden apples, they had a terrible shock. There was not a single apple on it. A thief had come in the night and stolen every one. The princesses ran to tell their father, who was greatly upset at the news.

"Do not trouble yourself, Father," said the middle princess. "My sisters and I will stand guard under the tree tonight. I will hear the thief coming from a great way off."

"And I will slay him with my arrows," said the youngest princess.

"And I will sing a lament over his body." said the eldest princess.

That night the three princesses made themselves as comfortable as possible at the foot of the tree.

"We must be sure to stay awake." said the eldest princess.

At first the sisters were quite merry together, but as the hours passed they all grew drowsy. Soon they were fast asleep.

At the first light of dawn the princesses awoke in a fright. They looked at the branches of the magic tree and saw that the glittering apples were all gone. They had failed in their task. The King was crimson with anger.

"I should not have trusted you!" he raged. "You are all quite useless. I will guard the tree myself tonight. No sneaking thief will get past me."

When evening came the King stood under the magic tree. The princesses brought him cushions to sit upon but he refused them.

"I will not fall asleep at my post." he said scornfully.

Darkness fell and the full moon rose into the sky. Still the King stood firm. Around midnight he heard a strange sound. Great leathery wings were beating the air, getting nearer and nearer. A gigantic shadow fell across the moonlit courtyard and, to his horror, the King saw an enormous dragon.

So this was the thief who had stolen the golden apples! Never in his wildest imaginings had the King thought of such a thing. He began to wave his arms to scare the beast away. But it grabbed him in one of its scaly claws and uprooted the magic tree with another.

The noise awoke the three princesses, who jumped from their beds and ran down to the courtyard. But they were too late. They could only stand and stare as the terrible dragon carried the King and his magic tree away over the sea.

The brave princesses ran down to the shore and jumped in their little boat. The wind filled their sail and they followed the dragon with ease, for the middle princess could see him clearly.

"He is fifty miles away," she said, "I can hear the beating of his wings and smell his fiery breath."

The sisters sailed all through the night. Then, at sunrise, the wind left them and the sail drooped. Their little boat could not move. For some time they sat wondering what to do. Their boat was going nowhere and the dragon was almost out of the eyesight of the middle princess. Soon all would be lost.

"Never fear." said the eldest princess. She took up her fiddle and began to play, singing a song of wonderful sweetness. As the princess played and sang, a group of dolphins rose up from the water, charmed by the music and ready to give the sisters their help.

The princesses threw ropes overboard and the dolphins took them in their mouths, pulling the little boat behind them across the sea. In this way they travelled for many hours, managing to keep sight of the dragon until, at last, the wind returned and filled the sail.

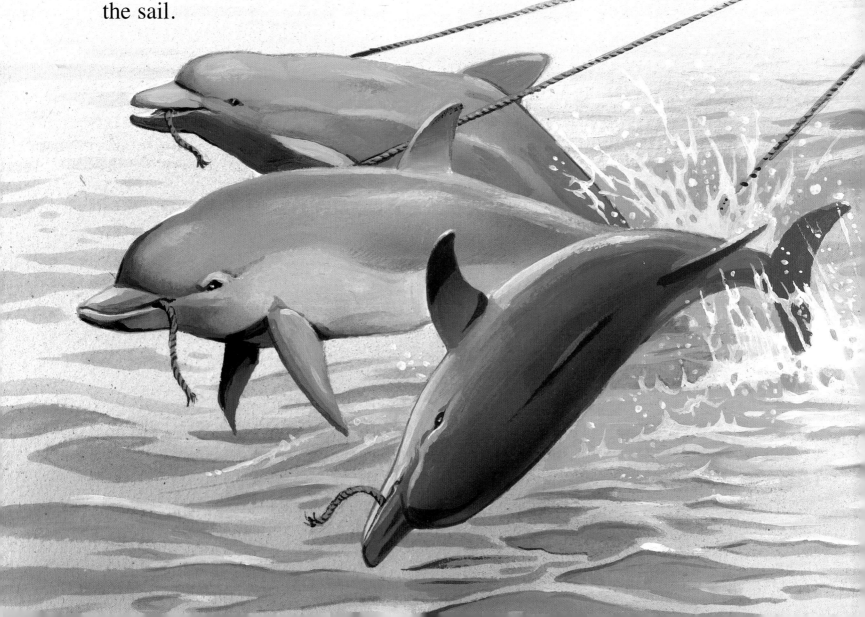

However, as soon as the dolphins had gone, a strange and eerie mist began to gather upon the sea. It swirled around the boat, thickening like a milky soup. Soon it was impossible to see beyond the front of the boat. The wind still blew, carrying them on but it did not blow away the peculiar mist. Even the eyes of the middle princess could not see through it, nor could she hear the far-off beating of the dragon's wings, for the mist muffled her ears like cotton wool. As for the smell of his flames, she could not catch a hint of it. There was nothing to do but sail on and wait for the mist to clear.

By noon the mist had lifted and through its last wisps the three princesses saw an enormous mountain of blood-red rock rising high out of the sea.

"I can hear the dragon breathing," whispered the middle princess. "He is in his lair somewhere in the heart of the mountain."

The sisters sailed their boat around the mountain, looking for a place where they might climb it. At last they found a narrow stairway winding up to the mouth of a tunnel far above them. They tied up their boat and began to climb. The way was dangerous, with nothing to hold on to, and the princesses took good care not to look down at the waves crashing below, in case they were overtaken by dizziness.

Inch by inch they moved forward until they reached the mouth of the tunnel. Now all three sisters could hear the dragon's breathing and smell his fiery breath. They crept through the tunnel into the heart of the mountain, until at long last the tunnel widened and they saw the dragon. It was curled up half asleep on its hoard of golden apples but one of its eyes was open and fixed on the King. He was chained up next to the transplanted magic tree.

When he saw his daughters the King's eyes filled with tears. He rushed towards them, but the chain around his ankle held him back. The key for this chain was kept in the dragon's mouth and the King was now its slave. The creature drew itself up, ready to burn the princesses to cinders.

"Wait a while," said the eldest princess quickly. "There is no need for haste, you can kill us whenever you wish. Allow me to play you some music and sing you a song."

The dragon loved music. It settled down and the princess began to play and sing.

> "Sleep, dragon. Sleep!
> The heavens are white with sheep,
> For they are lambs — those stars so bright,
> And the moon's the shepherd of the night.
> Sleep, dragon. Sleep!"

The dragon knew the song. It was an old lullaby that its mother had sung to it a thousand years ago. The princess's singing was sweetness itself and the enchanting music made its head swim. It closed its eyes and slept. Then, quiet as falling snow, the eldest princess crept up and stole the key from its mouth.

In a moment the sisters had freed their father from his chains. They ran back through the tunnel and picked their way down the mountain. The eldest princess quickly untied the mooring rope, while the middle princess set the sail.

However, in the dragon's lair a golden apple fell from the magic tree and tumbled to the floor with an echoing crash. The dragon awoke and let out a fearsome roar of anger that made the mountain shudder. It flew out of the cave and up into the sky, searching the sea with its cruel yellow eyes. At last it saw the boat and dived like an eagle upon a mouse.

"Now it is my turn to show my worth!" cried the youngest princess. She drew her bow and let fly an arrow. It flew straight and true, striking the dragon in its heart. The beast exploded into fiery red fragments, which fell like a shower of meteorites into the sea all around the boat.

The princesses sailed home with their father, who was completely changed by his adventure. He forgot his love of the golden apples and began to love his three brave daughters instead. And they all lived happily together in the castle by the sea.

The Twinkling Tailor

When a ball is held in fairyland,
The fairies dress up very grand.
They all compete for the finest dress,
They're all so eager to impress.
But the grandest dress you've ever seen,
Is always worn by the Fairy Queen.
She sends her Twinkling Tailor out,
To gather the twinkles from all about.
From rivers and brooks and bubbling becks,
He gathers the silver and golden flecks.

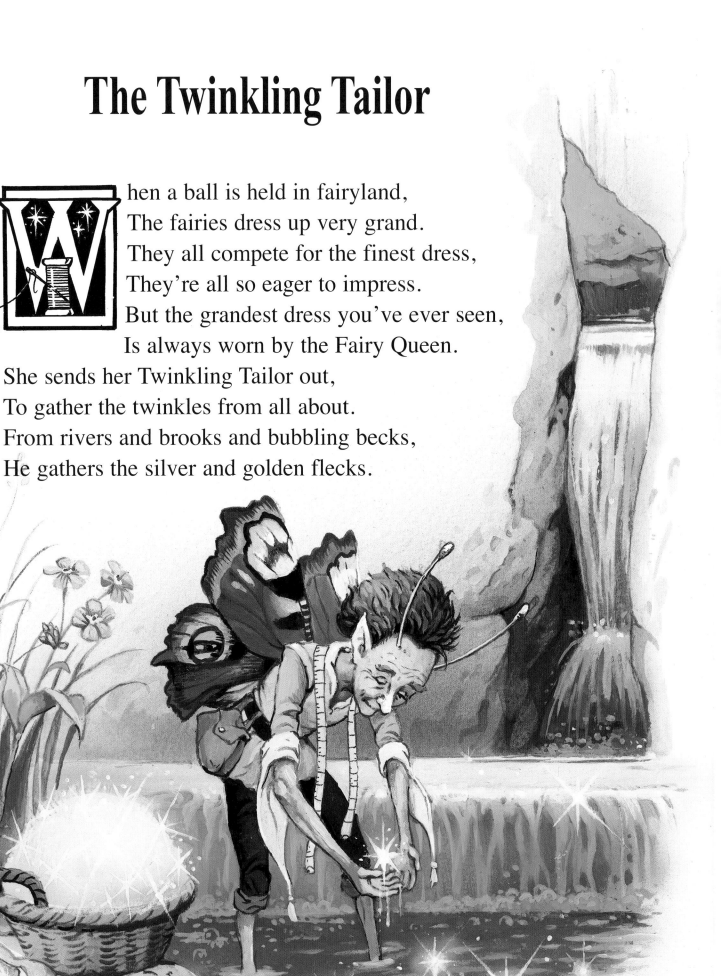

From the evening waves on sunset sands,
He scoops them up in his tiny hands,
Pink and orange, scarlet and blue,
Every colour and every hue.
Every twinkle from fountain and fall,
He gathers them carefully one and all.
Then the Twinkling Tailor in his tailor's shop,
Goes to work and will never stop
Until the twinkling dress is made,
For the Queen to wear in the fairy glade.
A dress so beautiful it seems
It could only be stitched from the threads of dreams.

13

The Enchanter's Daughter

ong ago in the magical Land of Light and Air, there lived an Enchanter and his beautiful daughter, the Weaving Maiden. All day long this maiden would sit at her loom, her shuttle flying backwards and forwards. Hour after hour, day after day, she sat weaving the bright blue cloth of the sky and the multi-coloured cloth of the shining rainbow. The Weaving Maiden would never for a moment leave her loom because of an ancient prophecy:

Sorrow, age-long sorrow shall come upon the world
When the Weaving Maiden leaves her loom.

The Weaving Maiden wore fine silken robes and jewels given to her by her father, but she did not care about such things. She was beyond happiness and sadness, knowing no desire but to weave. She neither laughed nor cried and nothing could distract her from her duty.

The Enchanter loved nothing more than to watch his daughter at work. He would stand for hours at her shoulder, delighting in the sight of the magnificent cloth pouring from her loom. But there came a day when the Enchanter put his hand upon the Weaving Maiden's shoulder and said, "Enough is enough. Leave your work now, my child. Make friends with the other young people. Be free and careless in the Land of Light and Air."

"That I cannot do," replied his daughter. "Have you not heard the ancient prophecy?

Sorrow, age-long sorrow shall come upon the world
When the Weaving Maiden leaves her loom."

"I know the prophecy," said the Enchanter, "but it means nothing. We are magical beings and prophecies have no power over us. Leave your loom."
But the Weaving Maiden just shook her head and continued to work.

Centuries passed upon the earth. Kingdoms rose and fell, but in the Land of Light and Air nothing changed. Not a single wrinkle marred the beautiful face of the Weaving Maiden.

Then, one bright morning, from over the shimmering horizon, a handsome Samurai prince came riding on a magnificent horse made of white cloud. He was the Prince of the Starry Night. His hair was as black as a raven's wing and his cloak was a deep, midnight blue, spangled with a million twinkling stars. He had come to court the Weaving Maiden, who gazed upon him and fell deeply in love.

The Enchanter's daughter left her loom. No longer the Weaving Maiden, her eyes shone brightly and she was always smiling. She went about the Land of Light and Air hand in hand with her Samurai prince, laughing and singing. The loom was forgotten as if it had never been.

At first the Enchanter was happy for his daughter, who bubbled with the joy of life. But as time passed he became worried. He stood at her loom and stroked his beard thoughtfully, remembering the ancient prophecy:

Sorrow, age-long sorrow shall come upon the world
When the Weaving Maiden leaves her loom.

It began to worry him and he grew angry.

"Who will weave the bright blue cloth of the sky and the multi-coloured cloth of the shining rainbow?" he asked. But his daughter laughed, shrugged her shoulders and danced away with her prince. Three times the Enchanter warned her, but each time she shook her head.

"No one can separate me from my love," she said.

"I am afraid you will find otherwise," said the Enchanter darkly. And he banished the Prince of the Starry Night, ruling that if he should ever return he would lose his life.

The Samurai prince rode sadly away on his horse of cloud and disappeared over the horizon.

"Give me back my beloved!" cried the Enchanter's daughter in great sorrow.

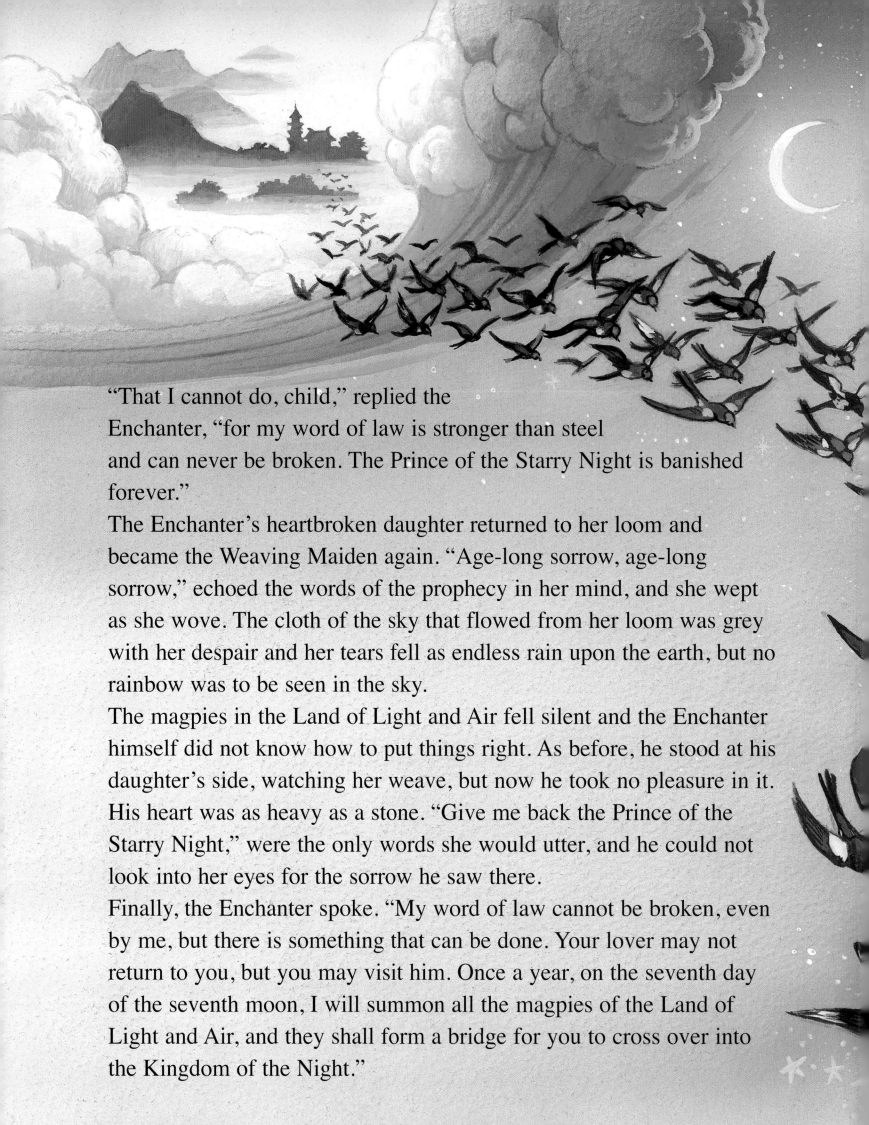

"That I cannot do, child," replied the Enchanter, "for my word of law is stronger than steel and can never be broken. The Prince of the Starry Night is banished forever."

The Enchanter's heartbroken daughter returned to her loom and became the Weaving Maiden again. "Age-long sorrow, age-long sorrow," echoed the words of the prophecy in her mind, and she wept as she wove. The cloth of the sky that flowed from her loom was grey with her despair and her tears fell as endless rain upon the earth, but no rainbow was to be seen in the sky.

The magpies in the Land of Light and Air fell silent and the Enchanter himself did not know how to put things right. As before, he stood at his daughter's side, watching her weave, but now he took no pleasure in it. His heart was as heavy as a stone. "Give me back the Prince of the Starry Night," were the only words she would utter, and he could not look into her eyes for the sorrow he saw there.

Finally, the Enchanter spoke. "My word of law cannot be broken, even by me, but there is something that can be done. Your lover may not return to you, but you may visit him. Once a year, on the seventh day of the seventh moon, I will summon all the magpies of the Land of Light and Air, and they shall form a bridge for you to cross over into the Kingdom of the Night."

So it was and so it always shall be, that on the seventh day of the seventh moon, the Weaving Maiden crosses over the bridge of magpies and runs into the arms of her love, the Prince of the Starry Night. When she returns she is filled with happiness. Then she once more begins to weave. The shuttle flies backwards and forwards, and the bright blue cloth of the sky and the multi-coloured cloth of the shining rainbow flow from her loom.

Adapted from a traditional Japanese fairy tale.

The Princess and the Unicorn

rincess Jasmine had everything a girl could dream of. The King's wife was dead and Jasmine was his only child. She was the light of his life. The princess only had to mention that she might like a new dress and the King would provide her with a dozen beautiful gowns of the finest silk and satin. She could hardly lift up her hands for the weight of the jewelled rings upon her fingers. But Jasmine was never satisfied. "Give the princess a silver carriage and she will wish for one of gold," whispered the palace servants.

When Princess Jasmine was almost thirteen years old, the King asked her what she would like for her birthday.

"I'm not sure, Father," replied Jasmine. "Something lovely and very expensive, I think. I'll sleep on it tonight and give you my answer in the morning."

The princess went off to her bedchamber and since she had nothing to worry about other than presents, she fell fast asleep as soon as her head touched her goose-feather pillow.

The night was warm and the princess had left her window open. As the full moon came out from behind the clouds it threw its shadows across the room. Moonshadows! Moonshadows that took on something of the shape of elves. They crept up to the sleeping princess's bedside and whispered into her ear. "If only you had a unicorn, how happy that would make you," they said. "A unicorn is what you would like for your birthday — nothing else will do. You must have a unicorn. You *will* have a unicorn!"

The following morning the princess went to find the King.

"Father, I know exactly what I want for my birthday," she said.

"And what is it, my precious?" asked the King, eager to please.

"A unicorn!" exclaimed Jasmine.

The King's face fell. "Oh, my dear, you know I would give you every star in the sky and every pearl in the sea, but I cannot give you a unicorn, for never in all my long life have I seen such a thing."

The princess became exceedingly angry. "I *will* have a unicorn!" she shouted. "I will!" And she stormed out of the room, slamming the door so loudly that a few flakes of ceiling plaster fell onto the King's head. Princess Jasmine could hardly believe what had happened. Her father had never said "no" to her before. How could he be so cruel as to deny her a unicorn? She flounced away through the gardens and out of the palace grounds, lost in a red fog of anger.

The princess walked without seeing where she was going, until she was brought to her senses by the sound of grunting and grumbling. A little man was struggling to free his long beard, which was trapped under a boulder.

"It happened while I was taking a nap here," explained the man. "Some of the boulders in these parts have a life of their own.

This one here just sort of rolled up and parked itself on my beard. Boulders have an odd sense of humour. Will you help me push it off, please?"

"Why should I?" said Princess Jasmine. She was still pretty cross.

"Because I ask you," replied the little man in surprise.

"That's really not good enough," retorted the princess. "What will you give me in return for my help?"

"Anything you wish for," said the man.

"Very well," said Princess Jasmine, and she leaned against the rock and began to push. The boulder did not move an inch.

"It's useless," she said sulkily, giving the boulder a kick.

"No need for that sort of thing," said the boulder in an offended voice, and it rolled over to one side. "Can't you take a joke?"

"There," said Jasmine. "You're free."

"Thank you," said the man, keeping an eye on the boulder to make sure it wasn't getting up to any more of its tricks.

"Now, what is it that you wish for?"

"I wish for a unicorn," said Princess Jasmine.

"No one can *give* you a unicorn," said the little man gravely.

"Unicorns must be caught by those who wish to possess them, but I have something that might help you." He handed the princess a small purse, filled with glittering dust. "When you find your unicorn," he said, "throw the dust into the air above his head and recite these words:

> *True like earth, true like air*
> *True like ice and fire.*
> *I cast my magic to the winds*
> *To catch my heart's desire.*

Oh, and by the way, you will find a unicorn somewhere in the middle of the deep, dark, dreadful forest, just over there." He pointed at the forest as the boulder began to inch its way towards him. "Must be going now," he said quickly, and away he went down the road, walking, jogging and finally running, with the boulder rumbling along at his heels. "Keep to the narrow path!" he called out as he disappeared around the bend.

Princess Jasmine walked confidently into the forest. "It
doesn't look in the least bit dark and dreadful to me," she
thought. The forest was light and airy and not at all frightening.
The narrow path wound between the silver birch and oak trees,
and the forest floor was carpeted with bluebells that danced in the
dappled sunlight. The princess walked along quite merrily.

Before long, though, the forest began to change. Princess Jasmine
was sure that the trees were closing in around her, although she never
quite saw them move. The air became heavy and she began to feel
incredibly tired. At last she sank down by the roots of a tree. She only
meant to rest for a while, but soon she was asleep.

As Princess Jasmine slept, darkness fell in the forest and the moon rose
above the tangled branches. Then the moonshadows appeared, flitting
between the trees. They slowly gathered around the princess and lifted
her gently up from the mossy ground.

"In the palace we have no power," they whispered, "but in the deep
forest our magic is strong. We have tricked her with the desire for a
unicorn that she will never see. We will carry her away to the land
of the moonshadows where the sun never rises."

But the moonshadows had waited too long. As if it had heard them, the sun rose and its first bright rays shone through the twisted trees. Touched by the sunlight, the moonshadows dropped the princess and fled, dissolving like smoke.

Princess Jasmine awoke with a jump. She looked around her. Where was the narrow path? It had disappeared and she was lost. She began to cry.

"Crying won't help," said a voice. A sleek red fox stepped out from behind a tree. "Crying never helped anyone. You can't see your path if your eyes are filled with tears. Here, take my handkerchief."

Princess Jasmine took the fox's handkerchief and dried her eyes. When she looked again, there was the narrow pathway, directly under her feet. The trees had spread themselves out again and the lovely sunshine slanted through them. The princess was filled with hope.

"Be on your way now," said the fox. "There is a clearing not far from here, where I think you will find what you are looking for."

Princess Jasmine handed the fox his handkerchief with a smile and a "thank you" and continued along the path. Soon she came to a clearing in the trees. The princess stood at the edge of the clearing and gazed in wonder.

In the clearing stood a unicorn, like a milk-white statue among the nodding wild flowers. He shone almost as brightly as the sun and Jasmine had to shade her eyes to look at him. His silvery mane and tail rippled on the gentle breeze. His long beard curved like that of a wise old wizard and the spiral horn upon his forehead was wreathed with daisies.

The princess took a deep breath and walked slowly toward the unicorn, who stood quite still. He knew that he could run faster than the wind, so

he had little to fear from a mere princess. Jasmine was no more than a yard away from him when she took the purse from her pocket and threw its contents up into the air. The glittering dust flew high up above the unicorn's proud head and the princess chanted the magic words,

"True like earth, true like air
True like ice and fire.
I cast my magic to the winds
To catch my heart's desire."

The dust transformed itself into a golden rope, which fell in a noose over the unicorn's neck. He was caught and could not escape. Princess Jasmine climbed on to his back, and at once he began to run. He ran faster than an arrow flying from a bow and the world around them became a blur of colour. He ran and he ran, until he could run no more and his heart beat inside him like a terrible drum. Then the beautiful unicorn fell among the tall grasses, exhausted and panting.
"Poor unicorn, what have I done to you?" sobbed Princess Jasmine. She stroked his elegant head and slipped off the golden rope. Then, to her amazement, the unicorn at once began to recover. He struggled to his feet and tossed his mane, and then he was gone. He ran as if he would never stop, on and on until he disappeared into the misty blue distance.
The unicorn had left Princess Jasmine out in the middle of nowhere.
If it had not been for the little man suddenly reappearing over the hill (with the boulder at his heels) she might never have got home. The princess spoke very sternly to the boulder and sent it on its way.
Then the man showed her the way back to the palace. They walked in silence, for the princess was lost in thoughts of the unicorn.

"Never try to tame a unicorn and it will always be your friend," the little man said as he left her at the palace gates.

That night Princess Jasmine dreamed that she was carried far away to enchanted places on the back of the unicorn. In the morning she awoke feeling sad. Would she ever see him again? But when she went to the window and drew back the curtain, he was waiting for her in the garden, gleaming brightly in the sunlight.

From that day on, Jasmine was a changed princess. She no longer demanded silk dresses and jewelled rings, for she had found a friend who meant more to her than all the possessions in the world. The unicorn visited her often and she was always pleased to see him, but she never forgot the little man's advice, and the unicorn remained as free as the wind.

The Dandelion's Time

When the dandelion was golden yellow
He listened with a sigh
To the secrets of the summer breeze
As she gently passed him by.
The fairies played around him
And he watched their fairy games.
He heard their tinkling laughter
And he knew all of their names.

When the dandelion grew old and grey
His head was filled with care.
The wind came dancing by him
And she blew off all his hair.
One o'clock, two o'clock
Three and four.
She blew his time far, far away
And the fairies came no more.

Molly and the Sorcerer Troll

Once upon a time, when the world was alive with magic and fairies, there lived a clockmaker and his daughter, Molly. The clockmaker's wife had died but the old man had done his best in bringing up his daughter and now she was almost a grown woman. Molly had long golden hair, a slender waist and a pretty face, and she was as good as she was beautiful. But the clockmaker's eyes were beginning to fail him and he could no longer see to make the tiniest parts of the clocks.

"The time has come when I can no longer support us," the clockmaker told his daughter. "You must go out into the world and look for some work for yourself."

Molly kissed her father goodbye and, with her few belongings tied up in a bundle, she set out on the road.

The girl had walked for a day or so when she arrived in a strange village. The streets were quiet and still and no one moved about on them. Molly felt uneasy. Still, she decided to try knocking on a door or two to see if anyone needed a maid. She tried many doors and peeped into many windows around the village but she found no one at home. The houses were silent and empty. At the blacksmith's a horseshoe and a hammer lay upon the anvil as if the smithy had been working there just a moment ago. In the baker's shop a loaf of bread lay half wrapped upon the counter, but it was as stale and hard as a brick. On the hill above the deserted village stood a grand castle. It looked dark and scary, but Molly needed work. She walked up the road to it, singing to herself as she went to keep her courage up. At last she reached the top of the hill and went to knock on the castle door. However, before she had raised her hand, the door was opened by a huge troll dressed in sorcerer's clothes.

"What do you want?" growled the troll.

"I'm going about the world to find work," answered Molly bravely.

"Do you wish to come and serve me?" the troll said, sounding surprised.

"Well, it might just as well be you as anyone else," Molly replied.

"Follow me," he said, and led her into the castle. "Your tasks are simple. You will cook and clean for me and you will feed my birds."

He led her to a golden cage in which a magpie was perched. The bird hopped over to see Molly, tilting its head from side to side in an inquisitive, almost human way. She liked it at once.

"You will feed this bird seed and give him water, nothing more," said the troll. Then he went to a casket on a high shelf and took out a set of keys. He unlocked a door and led Molly inside. "Step nimbly and close the door behind you," he told her. The room was an aviary, filled with hundreds of squawking, chattering birds. "These you will also feed," said the troll. "Come to me each morning and I will give you the keys. Make sure you close it when you leave."

Molly found the work was not too hard and she grew very fond of the birds. She especially loved the magpie in the golden cage. Though the troll gave her little to eat and had told her only to feed the bird with seed, she always managed to smuggle him tit-bits from her own plate and in the evenings she sang to him in her sweet voice.

One morning Molly was gathering herbs in the garden when she found a fieldmouse caught in the netting that covered the strawberries. The girl opened the net to let the mouse go.

"Thank you, Molly," said the mouse, and in a flash of light it changed into a lovely fairy with rainbow-coloured wings. "That was kind of you. It's high time you left the sorcerer troll. He is a wicked enchanter. Do as I tell you and all will be well. Go and free all the birds, especially the magpie in the golden cage, then come back to the garden."

The troll was out at the time, so Molly ran off quickly. By standing on her tiptoes on a chair she was able to reach up and take the keys from the casket on the high shelf. In a moment she had opened the door to

the troll's aviary and out poured the flock of birds. They flew once around the room and then out through the window and down into the deserted village, where they returned to their true shapes. They were human beings, free at last from the troll's enchantment.

Next Molly went to open the magpie's cage with the golden key, but at that moment she heard the troll returning.

Grabbing the cage, she ran down to the garden where a piebald pony was waiting for her. On the ground beside it was a stick, a stone and a pail of water.

"Hurry now," said the pony (who was the fairy in another disguise). "Pick up the stick, the rock and the pail of water and we will be off as fast as we can."

Molly got on the pony's back and away they went, up over the garden wall and down through the village, where the people cheered and waved.

After a time Molly looked behind. Just as she had feared, the troll was coming after her with great leaps and bounds.

"Throw the stick over your shoulder," said the pony. Molly did as she was told, and at once a thick bramble wood grew up behind them, blocking the road. But it did not delay the troll for long. He took an axe from his belt and chopped down the wood.

Molly looked back and saw that the troll was getting closer.

"Throw the rock over your shoulder," said the pony, and the rock went flying up into the air. Where it landed, a great mountain of granite appeared. But this was nothing to the troll. He took a huge hammer from his belt and smashed the mountain to smithereens.

Molly looked back again. The troll was very close behind them now.

"Throw the pail of water down," said the pony, "but mind you don't spill any of it on me."

Molly did as she was told, but a drop of water fell upon the pony's flank. Because of that drop, they were plunged into a deep lake. But the pony was strong and swam safely to land. Molly looked back for the last time and saw the troll splashing helplessly in the water. Then the lake closed over him and he was never seen again.

The piebald pony carried Molly all the way home to her father's house. There it left her and galloped away over the hills. After greeting her father with many kisses and hugs, Molly took the golden key on the troll's key ring and unlocked the magpie's cage. The bird hopped out at once, and there and then returned to what it had once been – a tall handsome prince in black-and-white robes.

The prince had fallen in love with Molly for her kindness and her sweet voice, and now she lost her heart to him. They were married and went to live in the castle on the hill, which had belonged to the prince before the sorcerer troll had taken it from him. Molly's father was well cared for and loved to the end of his days, and the prince still cocked his head on one side when he was listening to Molly singing, just as he had when he was a magpie.

Friend or Foe

If you are wise and knowing
You will be the fairies' friend,
Your crops will grow, the seeds you sow
The fairyfolk will tend.
Your stream will flow with water
So sweet and cool and clear,
And to your door will come no more
The troubles you may fear.
If you are cruel and heedless
You will be the fairies' foe,
Your plans will fail, the baby wail
And life be filled with woe.
Misfortune will come knocking
Mis-chance will let her in,
No use to cry, the rose will die
Your cattle all grow thin.
So be a friend to fairies
And they'll be friends to you,
Leave out a treat, some food to eat
Each night the moon is new.

Dancing for the West Wind

nce upon a time there was a seamstress with a touch of magic about her. The magic got into the clothes she made, so she was never short of work to do. But she had no children and this made her very sad. Sometimes she would lay down her needle and thread and imagine how lovely it would be to have a child to care for. To feel its little arms around her neck and have its smiles and laughter to brighten her days.

The seamstress often went walking in the hills around her house. She loved the wildflowers that grew among the trees there. One morning when she was taking a walk she began talking to herself. "If I only had a baby," she sighed. "How sweet life would be. No child in all the world would be better loved than mine."

The poor woman sighed so unhappily that it touched the soft heart of the West Wind, who was busy rustling the leaves in the trees. He blew down from the clouds and delivered a baby girl into the woman's arms.

"The child is yours to love and care for until she is twelve years old," said the West Wind. "But then I will return to claim her. See that she learns to dance. I love to pluck the leaves from the trees and see them dancing in the bright air. To watch a child dance would be so much better."

The woman was overjoyed. She named the baby Klara and loved her dearly. As soon as Klara was old enough, she began learning to dance. She was a very good pupil, and so graceful that her feet hardly seemed to touch the ground.

The years sped by and the seamstress's life was filled with happiness. She forgot all about the pact she had made with the West Wind.

On Klara's twelfth birthday the girl was out among the trees on the hillside, picking flowers for a daisy chain. Suddenly the leaves around her began to swirl and dance and the West Wind spoke in her ear. "Go home to your mother, Klara," he said. "Remind her of the bargain she made with me."

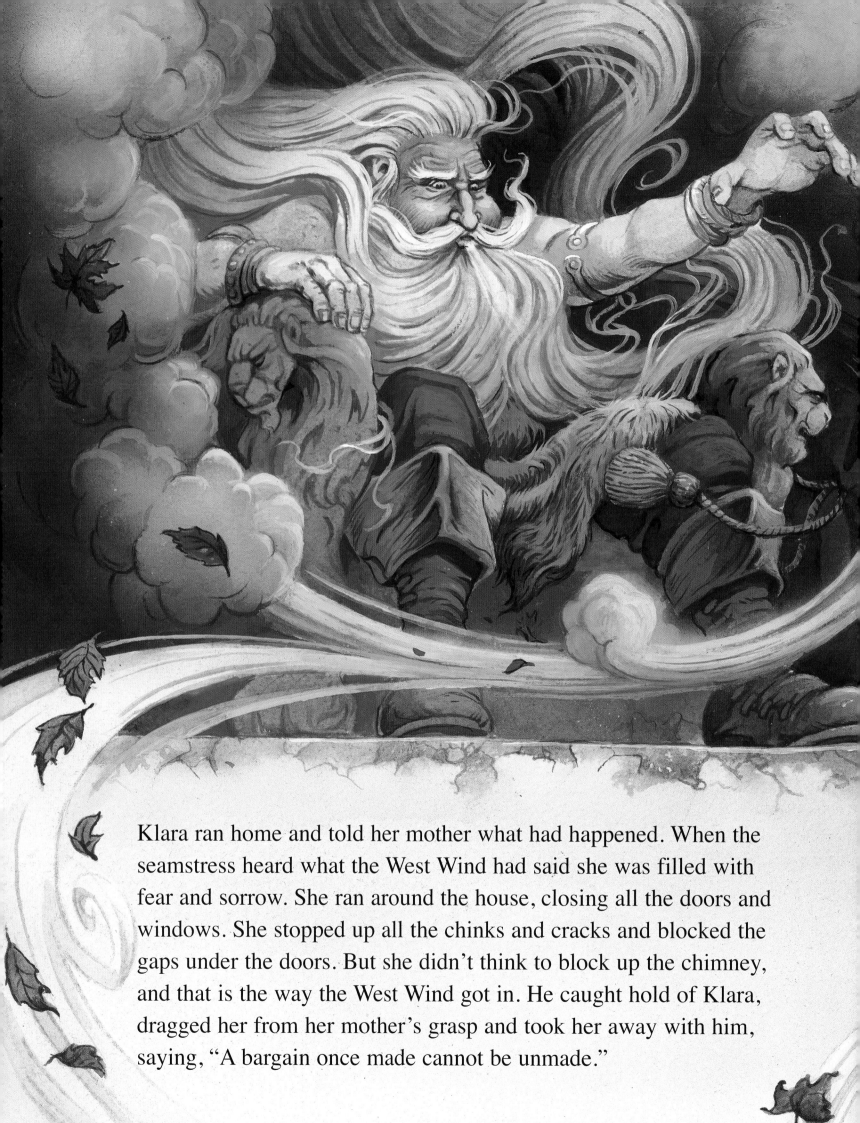

Klara ran home and told her mother what had happened. When the seamstress heard what the West Wind had said she was filled with fear and sorrow. She ran around the house, closing all the doors and windows. She stopped up all the chinks and cracks and blocked the gaps under the doors. But she didn't think to block up the chimney, and that is the way the West Wind got in. He caught hold of Klara, dragged her from her mother's grasp and took her away with him, saying, "A bargain once made cannot be unmade."

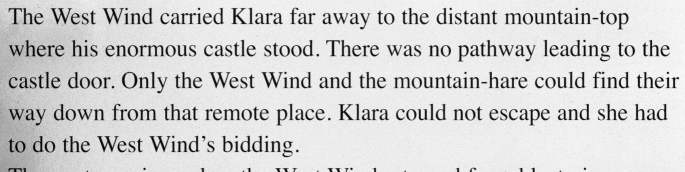

The West Wind carried Klara far away to the distant mountain-top where his enormous castle stood. There was no pathway leading to the castle door. Only the West Wind and the mountain-hare could find their way down from that remote place. Klara could not escape and she had to do the West Wind's bidding.

The next evening, when the West Wind returned from blustering around the world, he asked Klara to dance for him. Her dancing was exquisite and it pleased the West Wind very much. The hall in which she danced was filled with autumn leaves that blew forever around in circles and the girl swirled and whirled among them as if she herself were a leaf.

But after a while the West Wind noticed that her steps seemed heavier than before. Then she began to weep.

"What is the matter, child?" he asked.

"These leaves break under my dancing feet as my mother's heart must be breaking at the loss of me," she cried. A tear came to the West Wind's eye, and he told the girl that she need not dance any more that night.

The following evening, when the West Wind asked Klara to dance, she could only manage a few steps before she sank to the ground, looking pale and sad.

"The leaves that blow hither and thither about this hall remind me of my poor mother," she sighed. "She will at this moment be running about the hills searching for me all in vain."

Another tear came to the West Wind's eye, and again he told Klara that she need not dance any more that night.

On the third evening Klara looked around the hall at the brown autumn leaves and hung her head. "The leaves are dying because the summer is over, just as my mother will die of sorrow because I have gone."

At this the West Wind shook his head sadly and said, "This will never do, Klara. I am no ogre and I cannot bear to see you so unhappy. You must return to your mother." He summoned the mountain-hare to him. "Will you take Klara home to her mother?" he asked. "I am weary and no stronger than a breeze. I cannot carry her."

"Yes, I will take her," replied the hare. Klara said goodbye to the West Wind and followed the hare down the treacherous mountainside.

They had not gone very far when the North Wind saw them. Taking a fancy to Klara's pretty face, he decided to snatch her up and carry her away with him. But the mountain-hare was sharp-eared and he heard the North Wind coming.

"Quick, Klara!" he said. "Quick as you can! Hide with me."

They squeezed into a tiny crevice in the rock and peeped out. Although he ranted and raged, the North Wind could not reach them. He tore at the rocks with his icy fingers and threw snow and hail at them, but it was no good. Finally he gave up and went away, howling like a wolf over the mountainside.

Klara and the hare came out from their hiding place and continued on their way. But a little further on, the South Wind sidled up next to Klara. He was not at all like his rough brother. He whispered softly into the girl's ear, hoping to lure her away with his charm.

"Come with me," he said gently. "I will carry you to far away places where the sun always shines, olive trees grow and the sea is sapphire blue."

"Don't listen to him," said the hare. "Put your fingers in your ears, Klara, or else he will enchant you with his voice. He will whisk you away and you will never see your mother again."

Klara did as the clever hare told her. And before long the South Wind stopped whispering and blew away.

Klara scrambled a little further down the mountain until she saw the roof of her home and a thin wisp of smoke curling up from the chimney. But just then the East Wind came tearing through the trees, his arms outstretched to grab her.

"Quickly! Unwind your sash and use it to tie yourself to this pine tree!" cried the hare. Klara bound herself to the tree and the hare hid in its roots. The East Wind tore at the girl's clothes and pulled her hair for all he was worth, but he couldn't loosen the sash. At last he seemed to have given up and gone. But as soon as Klara untied herself, he turned around and came storming after her.

Klara and the hare ran for her house as fast as their legs would carry them, but as they were running in through the front door the East Wind caught hold of the hare's tail and pulled it off.

The seamstress wept tears of joy and relief to see her daughter home safe and sound. Then, because the mountain-hare had been so brave and clever, and because she had that bit of magic about her, she made him a new silver tail and stitched it in place.

Klara grew to be a beautiful young woman. She danced all around the world, entertained kings and queens and finally married a prince and lived happily ever after.

The Offended Brownie

nce upon a time in Ireland there was a cottage by a bog, where a clever woman lived with her idle husband and lazy daughter. She was always hard at work, but her family never lifted a finger to help her. Every day she milked the cow, fed the hens and collected their eggs. She tended the vegetables in her little garden and kept the house cosy and clean. Unfortunately her husband and daughter could hardly be bothered to get out of their beds.

One morning the woman was busy with her cooking when she heard "TAP TAP TAP" on the door. She opened it and saw a little man standing on her doorstep. He was wearing a rust-coloured cap with a white feather, a fur waistcoat and patched trousers, and his face was as brown and wrinkled as a nut.

"Will you give a brownie a bite of something to put between his teeth?" the little man asked. "I'm so hungry that I could eat a horse."

The woman felt sorry for the brownie and invited him in. "Sit by the fire and help yourself to the stew in the pot," she told him with a smile.

The brownie did not need to be told twice. He ate up every bit of the stew, wiping the last of the delicious gravy up from his plate with a piece of home-made bread. When he had finished, the brownie thanked the woman for the stew and went on his way.

At midday the idle husband and the lazy daughter got out of bed. They sat down at the kitchen table, even though it was too late for breakfast and too early for dinner.

"I'm hungry," whined the lazy daughter.

"Can I smell stew?" asked the idle husband.

"The pot is empty," said the woman. "I made a lovely stew but a brownie ate every last bit of it."

The husband and daughter could not believe their ears. They went straight back to bed, cross and hungry.

The next day was market day. Early in the morning the woman shook her daughter awake and asked her to stir the stew that was bubbling on the stove. Then she set off with her basket full of eggs to sell. The day was fine and bright and she sang as she walked down the path.

Back at the little cottage by the bog, the stew was filling the kitchen with a mouth-watering smell and the lazy daughter was dozing with her feet up on a stool, when she heard "TAP TAP TAP" on the door. "Come in," she called (she was much too lazy to go to the door). The brownie stepped inside.

"Will you give a brownie a bite of something to put between his teeth?" asked the little man. "I'm so hungry that I could eat a horse." "I certainly will not," snapped the daughter. "Be off with you!" And she hit him over the head with her mother's broom.

The brownie gave a loud screech and the broom was snatched out of the girl's hands. "Sweep her out!" shrieked the brownie, dancing with rage. "Sweep her out!"

The broom swept the girl all around the table and out of the door. It swept her through the garden, past the frightened chickens and up over the fence.

It swept her far out into the bog. Then the bog opened up under her feet and she sank into it, up to her neck and over, until not a bit of her was to be seen.

When the clever woman returned from market it was dark. She found no sign of her daughter and no sign of the stew.

"Where is our daughter?" she asked her husband. He just shrugged his shoulders. So as soon as the sun rose next day she went out to search, leaving her idle husband minding the house.

The man was sitting mumbling and grumbling to himself in the kitchen when he heard "TAP TAP TAP" on the door.

"Come in or go away – please yourself," he said.

The brownie opened the door and stepped inside.

"Will you give a brownie a bite of something to put between his teeth?" he asked. "I'm so hungry that I could eat a horse."

"Then go away and find a horse," snapped the man, rudely. "You'll get no food from me."

The brownie flew into a temper. "Up poker and beat him!" he shrieked. The poker by the fireside leapt into the air and began to beat the man about the shoulders.

It beat him all around the kitchen and out of the door.

It beat him through the garden, past the frightened chickens and up over the fence.

It beat him far out into the bog.

The woman was on her way home and saw her husband being chased by the poker. She watched as the bog opened up beneath him and he disappeared into it, closely followed by the poker and the furious brownie. The clever woman was very upset. Even though her husband and daughter were lazy, she loved them and she wanted them back. She sat down to think.

"The brownie must be very hungry," she said to herself. "Tomorrow I will cook a wild hare with carrots and onions and leave the kitchen door ajar. The brownie will smell it and come knocking. Then I'll ask him to bring my husband and daughter back to me."

But the offended brownie did not come back. For a month the woman cooked wonderful food to tempt him, but he ignored her. Then she remembered that brownies love sweet things. So she decided to bake a cake.

The clever woman baked a wonderful cake of rich golden brown. She filled it with nuts and cherries and raisins. She gathered violets with the morning dew still on them, then sugared them to decorate the edges of the cake. On the very top she put three sugared roses. It would make your mouth water just to look at it.

"If any brownie in the country can resist that cake," said the woman to herself, "then I'm the King of Ireland's daughter."

She took her best tablecloth and spread it out on the bog where her husband and daughter had been swallowed up. She put the beautiful cake in the centre of it. Then she sang:

"Come brownies here's a cake for you
The best in county Kerry.
It's topped with sugared flowers
And filled with nut and cherry."

No sooner had she finished the song than the brownie jumped up out of the bog, licking his lips at the sight of the cake.

"Take the cake. It's yours for the trouble of speaking a word," she said, holding it up under the brownie's nose. It was too much for the little man to resist. He put two fingers between his lips and gave a loud whistle. The bog around them began to shake and shiver and up from among the reeds came the clever woman's husband and daughter, surrounded by brownies.

The woman gave her cake to the brownies and turned to welcome her family home. When she looked around again the brownies were gone, and that was the last she ever saw of them.

The brownies had worked the idle husband and the lazy daughter hard, day and night, with never a moment to catch their breath. It had changed them forever. They were so happy to be home, they started to do their share of the work. The daughter milked the cow, fed the hens and collected their eggs. The husband tended the vegetables in the garden. The clever woman still kept the house cosy and clean, and cooked delicious meals. And when the evening came, all three sat together, tired and happy by the fireside, in the little cottage by the bog.